The Adventures of
Tundra Dog

P. Gail Holmes & Twila Everitt
Illustrated by Lynn Graham

Alazina Publishing
Anchorage, Alaska

*Across the tundra
in the great north land
lives a brave and fearless
squirrel.*

*He stretches and yawns
as he greets the dawn
to begin his journey with
the world.*

Stopping to whiff
a strange red sniff,
he grins and dreams
of flying.

Tundra Dog!
Tundra Dog!

"Beaver! Beaver!
Can you fly?"

"No! No!
I can't fly!
I build dams.
That's the reason why.

So run along
and enjoy your play
I'll see you
another day!"

"Mama Moose!
Mama Moose!
Can you fly?"

"No! No!
I can't fly!
I'm teaching my little ones,
that's the reason why."

"What about Daddy Moose?
Could he help me fly?"

"Oh! Yes!
We'll give it a try!
Climb up on my back,
then on to my rack!

Fly!
Tundra Dog
Fly!"

"Thanks, my friend!
I'll see you again!"

"Eagle! Eagle!
You can fly!
Would you mind
if I give it a try?"

Soar!
Tundra Dog!
Soar!

"With wings spread wide
and the world below
we will soar where
mountain sheep go."

"Looking down below
 from up so high
 it's so much fun
 'don't want to say goodbye!"

"Fly!
Tundra Dog
Fly!"

"Thanks my friend,
 I'll see you again!"

"Sheep! Sheep!
Are you aware?
I flew with Eagle
in the brisk morning air!

Sheep! Sheep!
You can't fly!
How will I get down
from up so high?"

"You'll never know
if I can fly,
until I show you...
Give it a try!

So, get on board
'cause we're headed down,
where the earth is level
and berries are found."

*"Thanks my friend
for bringing me back
to my very own
blueberry patch!*

Yummmmm..."

"Beavers can't fly!
Moose can't fly!
Sheep can't fly...
not really...

Neither can I!
Oh well...
(sigh)...

But, what's this?
Another strange smell?
On my very own
tundra trail?"

" I like adventure!
I like flight!

Fly,
Tundra Dog!
With all your might!"

"Whew!
That friend was mean!
He nearly caused
a very bad scene!

But, I'm sure
tomorrow's another day,
with more adventure
along the way!

So long for now
and always remember..."

*"Flying doesn't always have to be,
the way others see it... you see,*

*Just dream in your head!
Set your heart free!*

*You too can fly,
and be where you want to be!"*

*Tundra Dog!
Tundra Dog!*

Tundra Dog is a character
named after an arctic ground squirrel
that followed Gail and Lynn around Alaska
begging to be noticed.